Growing Readers

Mommies Say Shhh!

PATRICIA POLACCO

Mommies Say Shhh!

Philomel Books
New York

Birds say cheep, cheep, cheep.

Squirrels say chee, chee, chee.

Bunnies say nothing at all.

Dogs say buff, buff, buff.

Sheep say baa, baa, baa.

Geese say honk, honk, honk.
Bunnies say nothing at all.

Chickens say cluck, cluck, cluck.

Ducks say quack, quack, quack.

Goats say ma-a-a, ma-a-a, ma-a-a.
Bunnies say nothing at all.

Cows say moo, moo, moo.

Cats say meow, meow, meow.

Pigs say oink, oink, oink.

Horses say neigh, neigh, neigh.

Everyone says cluck cluck, honk honk, quack quack, moo moo, ma-a-a ma-a-a, buff buff, meow meow, baa baa, oink oink, neigh neigh, chee chee, cheep cheep. . . .

Mommies say shhh, shhh, shhh.
And bunnies say nothing at all.

Patricia Lee Gauch, editor

Published simultaneously in Canada.   Manufactured in China by South China Printing Co. Ltd.
Designed by Semadar Megged.   Text set in 20-point Goudy.   The illustrations are rendered in pencil and watercolor.
Library of Congress Cataloging-in-Publication Data
Polacco, Patricia.   Mommies say shhh / Patricia Polacco.   p. cm.
Summary: Animals make many different noises, but when they make too much noise, their mommies quiet them down.
[1. Animal sounds—Fiction. 2. Domestic animals—Fiction. 3. Mother and child—Fiction.] I. Title.
PZ7.P75186Mo 2005   [E]—dc22   2004009459
ISBN 0-399-24341-0
1 3 5 7 9 10 8 6 4 2
First Impression